Dear Parent:
Your child's love of reading starts here!

Every child learns to read in a different way and at his or her own speed. Some go back and forth between reading levels and read favorite books again and again. Others read through each level in order. You can help your young reader improve and become more confident by encouraging his or her own interests and abilities. From books your child reads with you to the first books he or she reads alone, there are I Can Read Books for every stage of reading:

SHARED READING
Basic language, word repetition, and whimsical illustrations, ideal for sharing with your emergent reader

BEGINNING READING
Short sentences, familiar words, and simple concepts for children eager to read on their own

READING WITH HELP
Engaging stories, longer sentences, and language play for developing readers

READING ALONE
Complex plots, challenging vocabulary, and high-interest topics for the independent reader

ADVANCED READING
Short paragraphs, chapters, and exciting themes for the perfect bridge to chapter books

I Can Read Books have introduced children to the joy of reading since 1957. Featuring award-winning authors and illustrators and a fabulous cast of beloved characters, I Can Read Books set the standard for beginning readers.

A lifetime of discovery begins with the magical words **"I Can Read!"**

Visit www.icanread.com for information
on enriching your child's reading experience.

I Can Read!™

JUST A
TEACHER'S PET

BY MERCER MAYER

HARPER
An Imprint of HarperCollins*Publishers*

To Autumn and Tilly, our
favorite little Ninja Turtles

I Can Read Book® is a trademark of HarperCollins Publishers.

Library of Congress catalog card number: 2014959046
ISBN 978-0-06-207199-6 (trade bdg.) — ISBN 978-0-06-147819-2 (pbk.)
15 16 17 18 19 SCP 10 9 8 7 6 5 4 3 2 1 ❖ First Edition

A Big Tuna Trading Company, LLC/J. R. Sansevere Book
www.littlecritter.com

A new student comes
to our school.

Our teacher goes to
greet her.
We sneak a peek.

"Here they come," I say.
"Quick, everyone
sit back down."

We all say hi.
Then she gives
Miss Kitty an apple.

That is weird.

No one else does that.

She sits in the front desk.

Nobody wants to sit there.

She raises her hand first.

She passes out work sheets.

She turns in her class work first.

The bell rings. Class is over.
Time to go home.

Bunella stays.

She cleans the blackboard.

She's going to miss the bus.

We wait for the bus.

We get on the bus.

The bus doesn't move.

The bus waits for Bunella.

She was helping the teacher.

She must be the teacher's pet.

The bus takes us home.

Tomorrow we have a class trip.

We go to the museum.

Bunella tells us where to stand.

She reads our names.

We have to say "Here!"
What a teacher's pet.

Bunella watches us like a hawk.
"Don't touch that, and watch
where you are going," she says.

Time to go back to school.

We all stand in line.

Bunella counts us one by one.

We go to the auditorium for
a program. We are too noisy.

The teacher's pet says,
"Hush!"

Today ends early.
We have a ball game
with the older grade.

They always beat us.

But at least the teacher's pet can't tell us what to do.

"Don't forget to invite your new classmate to play," says Miss Kitty.

Bases are loaded.

It is Bunella's turn to bat.

I close my eyes.

Wow, Bunella hits a home run.

We win the game by one run.

She may be the teacher's pet,
but we all want her on our team.